THIS BOOK BELONGS TO:

_____

This paperback edition first printed in 2013 by Andersen Press Ltd.

First published in Great Britain in 2012 by Andersen Press Ltd.,
20 Vauxhall Bridge Road, London SW1V 2SA.

Published in Australia by Random House Australia Pty.,
Level 3, 100 Pacific Highway, North Sydney, NSW 2060.

Colour separated in Switzerland by Photolitho AG, Zürich.

Printed and bound in Singapore by Tien Wah Press.

Christopher Corr has used gouache in this book.

10   9   8   7   6   5   4   3   2   1

British Library Cataloguing in Publication Data available.

ISBN 978 1 84939 312 6

For Libby. S.D.

For Nick and Steve. C.C.

The Goggle-Eyed Goats

Stephen Davies   Christopher Corr

ANDERSEN PRESS

Old Al Haji Amadu lived in a town called Timbuktu in a very hot country called Mali in the middle of Africa.

He had THREE wives called Fama, Rama and Sama. He also had SEVEN children called Ali, Alu, Fati, Faruk, Halima, Talita and Zamp.

In his herd Al Haji had ONE dangle-tailed donkey, TWO snaggle-toothed camels, THREE curvy-horned cows, FOUR wobble-legged lambs and FIVE goggle-eyed goats.

Al Haji loved his goggle-eyed goats but they were extremely naughty.
Every morning they jumped out of their pen and went looking for things to eat.

They raided Al Haji's pumpkin patch, they gobbled Rama's radishes.

They chewed on Sama's patterned skirts . . .

. . . and munched on Fama's woven mats.

One day Fama, Rama and Sama went to Al Haji Amadu
and said, "ENOUGH! Those goats have got to go!"

Al Haji Amadu loved his wives more than he loved his goggle-eyed goats.
"Very well," he said, "I will take the goats to Mopti market and sell them."

"NO!" cried Ali, Alu, Fati, Faruk, Halima, Talita and Zamp, and they all began to talk at once.

"Please, please, please, please, please, please, please," said the children. "Please don't go to Mopti market. Don't get rid of the goggle-eyed goats!"

Al Haji Amadu raised his hands. "ENOUGH OF THE HULLABALOO!"
he said. "THE GOATS HAVE GOT TO GO!"

Early next morning Al Haji Amadu set off with the
goggle-eyed goats on the track to Mopti market.

The track was long and lonely, with nothing much to look at.
Nothing but sand dunes and thorn trees.

All day and all night old Amadu walked, and the flock of goggle-eyed goats grew more and more frightened.

"Meh meh meh meh meh," went the goats. "Please don't take us to Mopti market. Don't get rid of us goggle-eyed goats!"

At six o'clock in the morning Al Haji Amadu arrived at Mopti market.

His ears were met with the mooing of cows, the baaing of sheep, the braying of donkeys and the cluck-cluck-clucking of hens. Al Haji stood in the goat pen and waited for someone to come and buy the goggle-eyed goats.

Suddenly a boy popped out from the crowd. Al Haji Amadu's mouth dropped open and his eyes became as goggly as a goggle-eyed goat.

"ZAMP! WHAT ARE YOU DOING HERE?"

"Please don't be angry," said Zamp. "I followed you to Mopti market. Don't get rid of the goggle-eyed goats!"

Then out from the crowd popped Ali, Alu, Fati, Faruk, Halima and Talita. Al Haji Amadu goggled again.

"Please, please, please, please, please, please don't be angry," said the children. "We followed Zamp to Mopti market. Don't get rid of the goggle-eyed goats!"

Al Haji Amadu raised his hands. "ENOUGH OF THE HULLABALOO!" he said. "Your mothers don't like the goggle-eyed goats, so the goats have got to go."

Out from the crowd popped three women.
Al Haji Amadu goggled again.

"FAMA! RAMA! SAMA!
WHAT ARE YOU DOING HERE?"

"I had a change of heart," said Fama, "so I followed the children to Mopti market. Don't get rid of the goggle-eyed goats!"

"I found I missed the goats," said Rama, "so I followed Fama to Mopti market. Don't get rid of the goggle-eyed goats!"

"A goat-free life is dull," said Sama, "so I followed Rama to Mopti market. Don't get rid of the goggle-eyed goats!"

Al Haji Amadu raised his hands. "ENOUGH OF THE HULLABALOO!
We'll buy the goggle-eyed goats some grain and return to Timbuktu."

So Al Haji led the way home, followed by his THREE wives, his SEVEN children and his FIVE goggle-eyed goats. They walked all night and all day . . .

. . . and at last they arrived in Timbuktu. Waiting to greet them were **ONE** dangle-tailed donkey, **TWO** snaggle-toothed camels, **THREE** curvy-horned cows and **FOUR** wobble-legged lambs. But when **Old Al Haji** turned to count his **FIVE** goggle-eyed goats . . .

... he was in for a
BIG SURPRISE!

Also by Stephen Davies and Christopher Corr

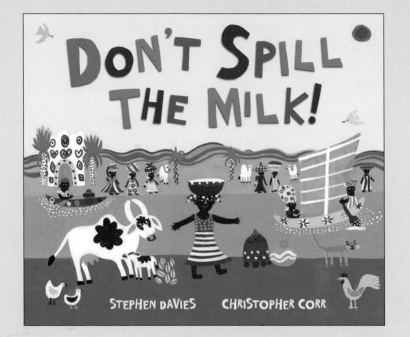

978 1 84939 452 9

Praise for The Goggle-Eyed Goats:

'One of the best new picture books of this year.'

The Times

'Strikingly bold and vibrant illustrations bring the market place in Timbuktu vividly to life.'

Julia Eccleshare